WAYLON'S WAY

A GHOST WALKER SHORT STORY

ALEXANDRIA BLAELOCK

BlueMere Books
MELBOURNE, AUSTRALIA

For permission requests, please contact
enquiries@bluemerebooks.com.

Ordering Information:
Discounts are available on quantity purchases. For details, contact orders@bluemerebooks.com.

Waylon's Way/Alexandria Blaelock
paperback ISBN: 978-1-925749-88-5
digital ISBN: 978-1-925749-89-2

WAYLON'S WAY

Sleeping in a ditch is mostly okay. The trench makes it hard for others to see you, especially at night, plus it offers an amount of protection from the elements.

Especially when it's a ditch under a hedgerow.

Hedgerows can be challenging to get into, especially when there's a lot of bramble, but on the plus side, brambles also give you something to eat. Bed *and* breakfast, you might say.

But if you can fight your way through the bramble, the ones who feel justified chasing you aren't likely to follow.

They might just throw a few rocks in your direction and leave it at that.

As far as they're concerned, you're just not worth that much aggravation.

Bramble thorns dig deep, which makes them difficult, as well as painful to remove.

Lots of digging around with fire heated needles in an attempt to prevent the wounds from festering.

But as far as Waylon, in his stolen leather coat was concerned, well worth the effort of wriggling down inside the border.

It's really only when it rains that ditches become a problem, because ditches are basically a way to collect and redirect water.

And if you're misfortunate enough to be in a ditch when it starts raining, well then, you're soaked through before you're even fully awake.

Most likely followed by death from pneumonia shortly thereafter.

Giving you the opportunity to join the ghosts that live all around you, and which normal people can't see.

The seeing of them is in the blood, only it doesn't come on you until puberty, and unless you happen to be near a Goist temple you've got to learn to deal with it on your own.

Waylon was an apprentice tailor when the ability manifested in him.

At first, he didn't know what he was seeing.

It was just that the Master's workroom all of a sudden got really crowded.

He didn't think much on it mind you, with the Spring wedding season coming up there was a lot of work on.

The Master brought in extra journeyman tailors every year, and with the Lady Marjery due to marry Prince Indulf that year there were a lot of people wanting new clothes for the Royal festivities.

So, it wasn't really surprising that there seemed to be a lot more tailors than was usual.

And as the Master wasn't the kind that tolerated chatter in his workroom, there wasn't much point trying to find out more about the journeymen.

Neither was he the kind that tolerates questioning from apprentices, not even the ones about take their final journeyman examinations.

Given Waylon was a foundling, he'd been more or less sold by the Church to the Master.

He owned nothing, not his name, and not even the basket he was found by the roadside in.

So, with nowhere to go, and no money to get there anyway, he rarely left the workshop.

But he'd worked hard, and thanks to his Master, was lucky to be permitted to sit the exams, and even more to have permission to journey after.

In fact, he'd fully expected to be returned to the Church as a sort of high-class not quite slave tailor once he'd completed his apprenticeship.

The Church did not believe in ghosts.

Except when it did, and then the people who claimed to see them were condemned to die horrible deaths as a warning to others.

The people who could really see them were called Ghost Walkers, because they could see and talk with ghosts, and come away unharmed.

People who appeared to talk to themselves were sometimes accused of being Ghost Walkers, and if they couldn't prove they weren't, were executed.

I'm sure you can imagine how well that went - it's harder to prove you aren't something than you are.

Not to mention that villagers and townspeople usually saw Ghost Walkers as the cause of all ill within the community, so they were more likely to be chased out or stoned to death before the Church got wind of them.

Hard to say which was the worst fate, both were likely to be brutal deaths, but at least the villagers were ruthlessly efficient and you died quicker.

A mercy I expect.

In any case, people were generally very careful about not talking to themselves, or other people who weren't readily visible.

For example, were inside buildings or on the other side of doors. You really couldn't be too careful when your life was on the line.

So Waylon, smiling quietly, eavesdropped on the journeyman's whispered conversations, and assumed that everyone else was doing the same.

It wasn't until he graduated to journeyman himself that he found out he was the only one who could see and hear them.

The Master called the workroom to attention, "Our Waylon here, has passed his exams and is now recorded in the Guild Register as a journeyman."

The room erupted with cheers and stamping feet, and he'd blushed with pride and pleasure, and beamed at the cheerleader.

Who'd looked surprised.

But when Waylon looked around at his fellow apprentices, he realised they weren't cheering or stamping.

They stood silently, hands tightly clasped in front of themselves, Heads bowed slightly, not meeting his eyes.

It was all a bit confusing.

He'd tried to focus on what the Master was saying, as he accepted a leather backpack to hold his new tools of trade; shears, measuring stick, pins and needles, thimble and chalk.

But he couldn't quite get his head around the ghostly celebration, and didn't know what to do about it.

Or how to thank the Master.

He knew journeyman apprentices with families usually took the Master's family out for a meal of thanks, but he had nothing but his thanks to share.

Partly for his education, and partly for not being returned to the Church.

The Master even gave him a coin and a bracelet to be going on with, and before he knew it, he was unemployed, on the street side of the firmly closed workshop door.

Expected to journey for three years and a day, calling no place home, but learning to work for anyone who could afford to buy the materials and pay for his services.

It was *very* exciting, though if we're being honest, Waylon was terrified as he took those first few steps out on his own.

He gained the reputation of being a bit peculiar, but the quality of his work was so fine the townsfolk he met along the way were prepared to ignore his peculiarities.

The way he got so much done each day.

His strange preferance for leaving town to sleep in ditches before returning for breakfast the next day.

That he barely said a word to anyone; only discussing garment form and function with himself, grunting measurements and calculations and barking instructions on how to stand for fittings.

"He's been alone for too long," people said.

"Hedgerow tea's done for him," they agreed.

But secretly, they remained incredibly proud to be dressed by The Demented Tailor.

His clothes were always thoughtfully designed with pockets in places you wouldn't have thought you needed them until you did.

It was almost as if he made clothes for a future time only he could see.

And while they were never quite fashionable, they were never out quite of date either.

They never seemed to wear out, and long after he'd gone, some of them were still handed down three generations later!

Some people claimed to have clothes made by him, but you could always tell the real thing.

They had a kind of magic about them that lesser clothes didn't.

You're probably wondering what happened that he was living in ditches wearing stolen clothes, and it's a sad story.

As I said, when he left his Master, he was excited and terrified.

The Master had called him "Waylon" instead of "boy."

Other apprentices might have disdained the second-hand tools he was given, but Waylon knew they were the Master's own tools; ones he'd used for many years.

The tools probably knew more about tailoring than Waylon himself.

And even though it was traditional to get some money for now and a bracelet to convert to cash if need be later, it wasn't always gold.

Waylon understood that his Master was proud of him and wanted him to do well.

And Waylon vowed that he wouldn't let his Master down, and would make him proud.

When his journeyman years were over, his masterpiece was a tailored suit of soft leather.

On the one hand it was a very practical outfit for outdoorsmen of the game and groundskeeping varieties.

And on the other a beautifully made and really quite handsome suit that wouldn't actually be too much out of place in the Royal Court.

Perhaps not before the King, but you get what I mean I'm sure.

As you can imagine it created quite some debate about whether it was in fact a suit that met the requirements for admission to the Tailor's Guild or was a better fit for the Leather Workers Guild.

The debate raged for many months, and in the end the Tailors refused him Guild membership.

To say he was utterly devastated is an understatement.

He begged for his piece back, and even though they hadn't approved it, they refused to give it to him.

Or let him alter it.

Or let him submit another.

Calling him enraged, is also an understatement.

Even that early in his career he was known as The Demented Tailor, and that bunch of fat old men who ran the Guild were probably afraid he'd bring the craft into disrepute.

The way that all fat old men who achieve a modicum of power are threatened by the changes new ideas bring with them.

Aside from his old Master of course.

Did you know the Tailor's Guild doesn't permit apprentices to marry until they achieve membership?

Now by that time Waylon was stepping out with a girl from Shephurst, and they'd all thought his membership was a foregone conclusion.

So much so they'd set a date for the service and she was busy sewing her trousseau.

She wasn't happy to be told the wedding was postponed.

But poor Waylon.

She was surprisingly prepared to start looking for a new beau.

A new Master Tailor to add insult to injury.

It was traditional at that time for the Guild to hold a feast welcoming the new Masters.

They'd left Waylon alone with his Master, raging in the hall while they went around the corner to the tavern to celebrate.

Waylon was inconsolable, so his old Master hatched a plan to help him steal the suit back.

They found his masterpiece, and Waylon put it in his backpack.

But as they were leaving, he accidentally knocked over a candle stand and a low candle that wasn't properly out caught fire.

His Master waited a few minutes to give him a head start before he called for help, but it was too late and the building burned to the ground.

The Master tried to keep his name out of it, but the committee had already decided it was Waylon's fault and decided that he had to be found and punished.

It was after his first night in a hedgerow that Waylon swapped his clothes out and discovered exactly how practical his leather suit really was.

As if he'd known he'd need it one day.

He got away safety that time, and spent the next few years travelling and working. But despite his ghostly help, it was only a matter of time before the Guild caught up with him.

And this time they were determined he'd be done for.

It might be that one of his ghosts turned against him; I can't think of another way they could've caught up with him in the ditch he was hiding in.

Almost as if that ghost was standing above him telling the tailors where he was.

But while ditches are good for hiding, they are in no way good for escaping, so he was effectively trapped in a hole.

Every time he tried to get out, they beat him back with cudgels.

He tried to protect his fingers for as long as he could, but they can't really be protected from a determined stamping foot.

And once he'd lost his fingers, he'd lost his livelihood, and didn't see much point trying to evade his tormentors any longer.

He just gave up and let them beat him to death before lighting his body on fire.

Waylon stood beside his burning body, with his ghostly journeyman companions by his side.

And accepted their reassurances that life as a ghost wasn't that bad.

After all, he'd travelled with them since he'd found himself on the other side of his Master's workshop door.

And their advice had never led him astray before.

In any case, dead or alive, there was always a place inside his Master's workshop for him.

If he wanted it.

THE END

ABOUT THE AUTHOR

Alexandria Blaelock writes stories, some of them for *Ellery Queen's Mystery Magazine* and *Pulphouse Fiction Magazine*. She's also written four self-help books applying business techniques to personal matters like getting dressed, cleaning house, and feeding your friends.

As a recovering Project Manager, she's probably too fond of sticking to plan. She lives in a forest because she enjoys birdsong, the scent of gum leaves and the sun on her face. When not telecommuting to parallel universes from her Melbourne based imagination, she watches K-dramas, talks to animals, and drinks Campari. At the same time.

Discover more at www.alexandriablaelock.com.

BOOKS BY
ALEXANDRIA BLAELOCK

SHORT STORY COLLECTIONS

The Histories of Hayward Hall
Lovelorn, Lovestruck and Love at First Sight
Common or Garden Variety Heroes
Case Files of the Wilkinson Detective Agency
Unavoidable Fates

OTHER FICTION

That Love Nonsense

MS BLAELOCK'S BOOKS

Stress Free Dinner Parties
Signature Wardrobe Planning
Holistic Personal Finance
Minimally Viable Housekeeping
Planning a Life Worth Living

SELECTED SHORT STORIES